Little
Red Riding
Duck

written by Charlotte Guillain ☆ illustrated by Dawn Beacon

Raintree is an imprint of Capstone Global Library Limited, a company incorporated in England and Wales having its registered office at 7 Pilgrim Street, London, EC4V 6LB – Registered company number: 6695582

To contact Raintree please phone 0845 6044371, fax + 44 (0) 1865 312263, or email myorders@raintreepublishers.co.uk. Customers from outside the UK please telephone +44 1865 312262.

Edited by Daniel Nunn, Rebecca Rissman, and Sian Smith
Designed by Joanna Hinton-Malivoire
Original illustrations © Capstone Global Library Ltd 2013
Illustrated by Dawn Beacon
Production by Victoria Fitzgerald
Originated by Capstone Global Library Ltd
Printed in China

ISBN 978 1 406 25115 9
16 15 14 13 12
10 9 8 7 6 5 4 3 2 1

This book is also available as a big book with the ISBN: 978 1 406 25121 0

British Library Cataloguing in Publication Data
Guillain, Charlotte.
  Little Red Riding Duck. -- (Animal fairy tales)
  1. Children's stories.
  I. Title II. Series
  823.9'2-dc23

Characters

Little Red Riding Duck

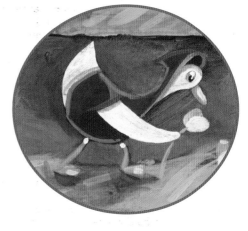

mother

grandma

wolf

woodcutter

Once upon a time, a little duckling lived
with her mother in the woods.

Her mother had made a red cloak for her, so everybody called her Little Red Riding Duck.

One day, Little Red Riding Duck's mother gave her a basket of food to take to her grandma's house.

Little Red Riding Duck was walking along the path when she met a wolf. "Where are you going with that basket of food?" he asked her.

"I'm taking it to my grandma's house," said Little Red Riding Duck, who was a little scared.

"You don't want to go that way,"
said the wolf. "I know a shortcut!"
But the wolf sent Little Red Riding
Duck further into the woods.

While Little Red Riding Duck was lost in the woods, the wolf ran ahead and knocked on grandma's door. When the old duck opened the door, he bundled her into a cupboard. "I'll save you for pudding," the wolf said, licking his lips.

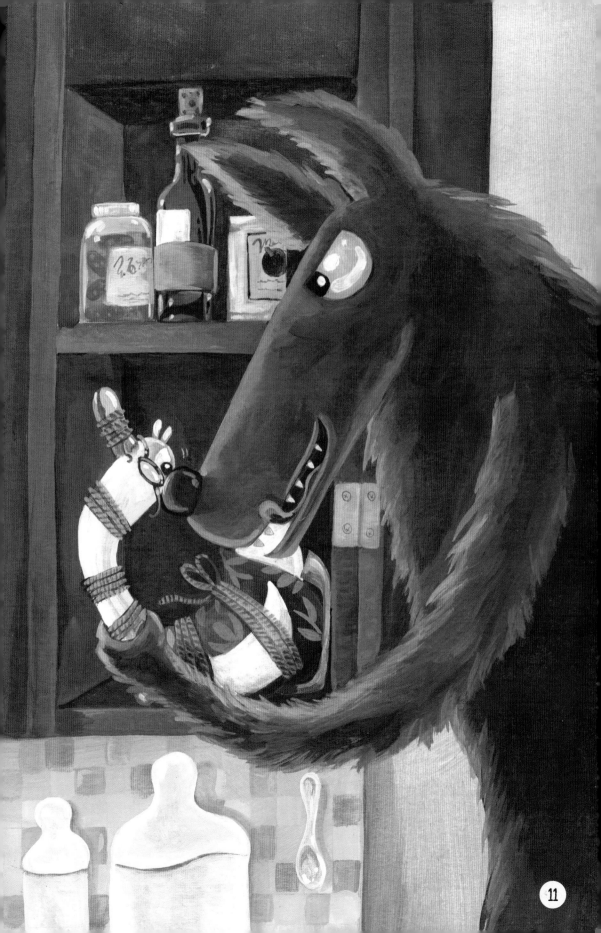

Then the wolf put on grandma's clothes and climbed into her bed. "When Little Red Riding Duck gets here, I'll be waiting for her," he chuckled.

Before long, Little Red Riding Duck knocked on the door and came in.

When she saw the wolf in her grandma's bed she gasped and said, "What big ears you have, grandma!" The wolf replied, "All the better to hear you with, my dear!"

Then Little Red Riding Duck said,
"What big eyes you have, grandma!"

The wolf replied, "All the better to see
you with, my dear!"

Finally, Little Red Riding Duck said,
"What big teeth you have, grandma!"

The wolf jumped out of bed and
replied, "All the better to eat you with!"

Little Red Riding Duck quacked loudly
for help. A passing woodcutter heard her
quacks, and came running to the rescue.

The wolf took one look at the
woodcutter's sharp axe and ran away as
fast as his wolfy legs could carry him.

Little Red Riding Duck, her grandma, and the woodcutter all sat down to enjoy tea together. And the wolf never bothered Little Red Riding Duck or her grandma ever again.

The end

Where does this story come from?

You've probably already heard the story that *Little Red Riding Duck* is based on – *Little Red Riding Hood*. There are many different versions of this story. When people tell a story, they often make little changes to make it their own. How would you change this story?

⁓⁓⁓⁓⁓⁓

The history of the story

The *Little Red Riding Hood* story was first written down by the Brothers Grimm. Jacob (1785–1863) and Wilhelm (1786–1859) Grimm lived near the city of Frankfurt, in Germany. They collected and wrote down many fairy stories and folk tales. These tales were told by oral storytellers who entertained people in the days before radio and television.

The original story is called *Little Red-Cap*. The girl is given a cap rather than a cloak with a hood and so she has a different name. She is sent by her mother to visit her sick grandmother and meets the wolf in the woods. The wolf suggests Little Red-Cap leaves the path to pick some flowers for her grandmother and this gives him time to run ahead to grandmother's house. When the wolf gets to her grandmother's house he eats her! Then he puts on her clothes and waits for Little Red-Cap. When Little Red-Cap arrives she notices the wolf's big ears, big eyes, big hands, and big mouth. Then the wolf eats her, too! The wolf falls asleep and snores loudly. A hunter hears the snoring and comes in to see if something is wrong. He thinks the wolf might have eaten the old woman so cuts open his stomach with a pair of scissors! Little Red-Cap and her grandmother come out, still alive. They fill the wolf's stomach with stones so when he wakes up and tries to run away he falls down dead. Everyone is happy and Little Red-Cap has learnt never to leave the path when she walks through the woods.